A-27295

E
BIR

Birchman, David F.

Brother Billy
Bronto's Bygone
Blues Band

$13.93

DATE		
2H	K-Sam	
MR 0 5 '93	MY 3 '96	
	Sa-a	
4 H	DC 22 '99	
APR 22 '93	AM-B	
J-DO	NO 10 '99	
JAN 1 2 '94	MR 21 '00	
K-Gol AM	Cmm	
MAY 0 3 '94	Sam	
K-S	NO 20 '01	
FE 0 1 '95		

Box 2A

© THE BAKER & TAYLOR CO.

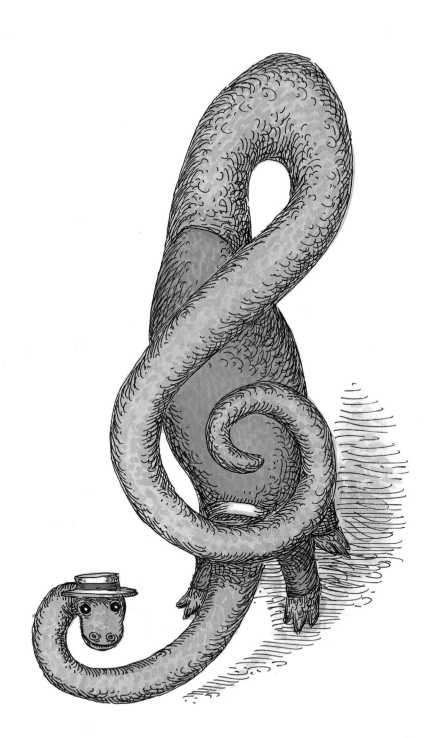

For Cole,
who taught his father
the difference between a sore ankle
and an ankylosaurus—D.F.B.

For Tess,   —J.O.

First Edition   1 2 3 4 5 6 7 8 9 10

Library of Congress Cataloging in Publication Data

Birchman, David Francis. Brother Billy Bronto's Bygone Bues Band / by David F. Birchman ;
illustrated by John O'Brien.
        p.   cm.   Summary: Brother Billy's dinosaur band is en route to a booking when their
train meets with a mishap in the bayou, where thereafter rests the blues in a pool of ooze. ISBN
0-688-10423-1—ISBN 0-688-10424-X (lib. bdg.)   [1. Dinosaurs—Fiction.   2. Bands (Music)—Fiction.
3. Stories in rhyme.] I. O'Brien, John 1953– ill. II. Title. PZ8.3.B53Br 1992 [E]—dc20
90-26114 CIP AC

Brother Billy Bronto's
Bygone Blues Band

BY DAVID F. BIRCHMAN

Illustrated by John O'Brien

Lothrop, Lee & Shepard Books   New York

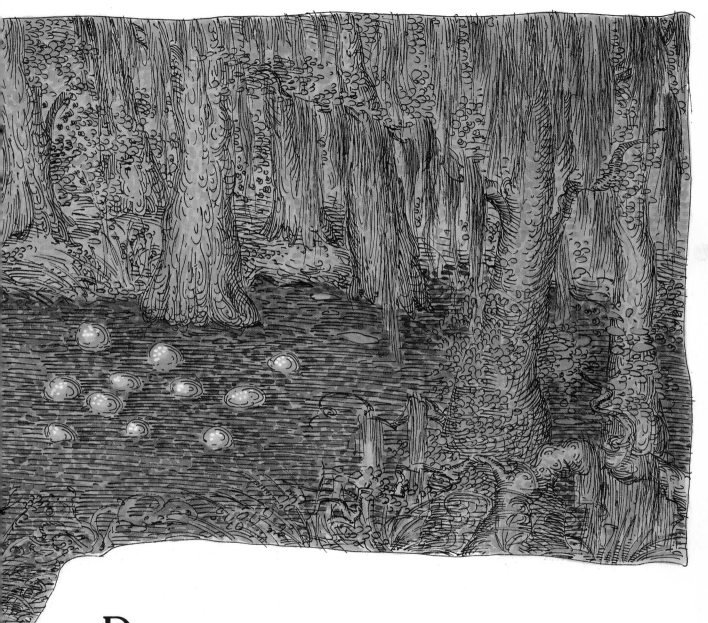

Deep dark down—I mean,
deep deep dark down in the bayou—
where the bones of the band in a jumble lie,
there rests the blues in a pool of ooze
with the ghosts of the bygone-bye.

Long ago when it was wondrous warm
and steamy swamps spread all across this land,
you could feel the heat off Basin Street
from Billy Bronto's Band.

Man, the place was a kitchen!
And that kitchen was hot 'cause the band was cookin'!

There was Rex the King Tyrone on the slide trombone
and Brother Billy on the bass.

There was a mean allosaurus saxophonist
nicknamed Lizard Lips Grace.

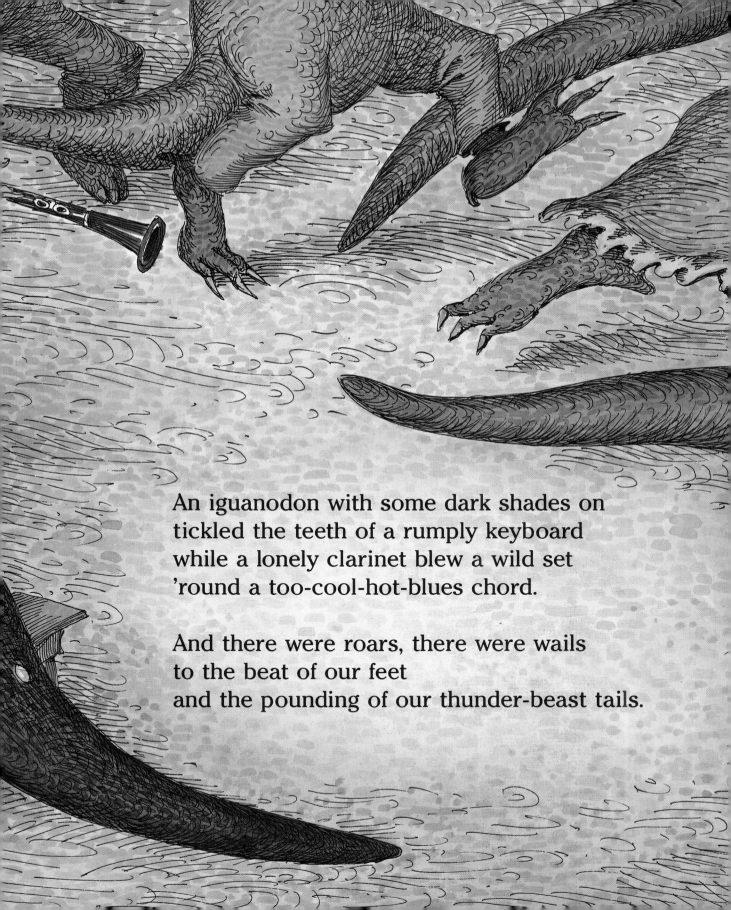

An iguanodon with some dark shades on
tickled the teeth of a rumply keyboard
while a lonely clarinet blew a wild set
'round a too-cool-hot-blues chord.

And there were roars, there were wails
to the beat of our feet
and the pounding of our thunder-beast tails.

'Course the heart of the band was the man.
Brother Billy. Brother Billy Bronto.
Thumping down on the big bass
with the rings on his claws all flashing bright—
They was dazzzlin'!—
Billy's gravely voice made the crowd rejoice
as it danced in the sultry night.

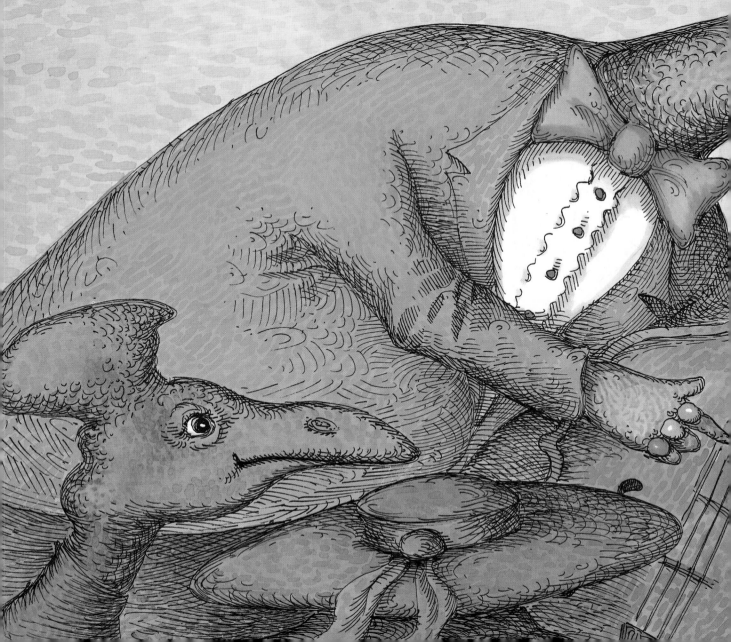

When Rex Tyrone slipped a loud clear tone
straight down the throat of his slide trombone,
it flowed down our spines just like hot turpentine
and it made all us dancin' beasts moan.

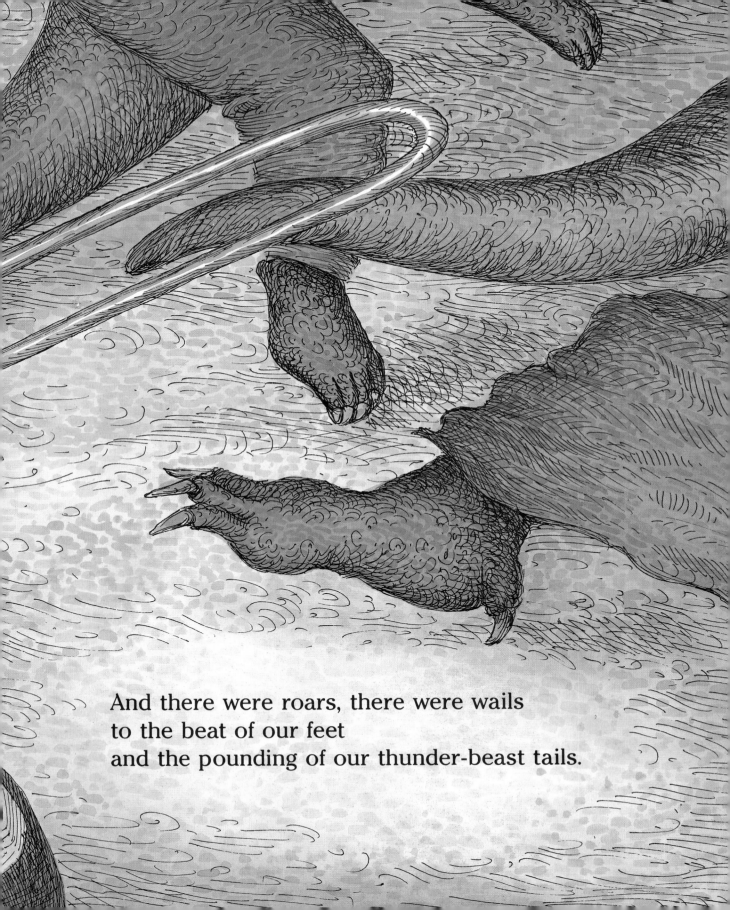

And there were roars, there were wails
to the beat of our feet
and the pounding of our thunder-beast tails.

A loud demand came from throughout the land
to hear the big beasts groove.
So tours were booked and the whole earth shook:
Billy's band was on the move.

They caught a train called the Red Ball Comet,
all bright red shiny and new,
and they took the blues down to Toopaloou
on the twisty tracks by the old bayou.

Son, that train was first class.
Billy's band didn't go unless it was first class.
I mean bright red shiny.
I mean chandeliers in the washrooms.
I mean plush thick carpets.
I mean deeeeeeeelux.

Those beasts jammed into those train cars
thick as jubblin'-bubblin' gumbo juice
with their brasses, basses, grinnin' faces,
and their long tails out the short caboose.

They were tooth to claw and snout to snout.
Their elbows popped all the windows out.
Talk about getting a table in the dining car
—Forget it!

It was a crowd-pleasing good-bye!
There was whoopin' and screaming, and streamers streaming.
There were best wishes, big sloppy kisses,
and a wet hankie in every eye.
Billy's band wouldn't leave unless there were wet hankies.

A whirling dervish trumpendous flourish
sent them sailing on their way,
as saxes blended into the raucous din
with a sound like burbling clay.

Then the train bumped and shuddered
And the tracks groaned with pain
When they all got going
        with the blues' smoke blowing.

The train went tssshick chatta-chatta-chatta
tssshick choo-choo

The band went romp stompa-stompa-stompa
boom bamm boom
tssshick-chatta-choo
boom bamm boom
boom-chatta   bamm-chatta
choo-choo-chooooooooooooooooooo

Hurtling down that railroad line,
the beasts in the band boomed on and on.
Faster and faster sped that blazing disaster
toward the bridge over Black Bayou Pond.

And there were roars, there were wails
to the beat of the band
and the rattle of the train upon the rails.

Let me tell you 'bout that bridge.
They was always going to fix it,
but they never got 'round to it.
And let me tell you 'bout that pond.
It was deep.

Where the old tracks twist through the bayou mist
roared that train a-rocking and shaking.
The band was smokin' with the throttles wide open
and it had no mind for braking.

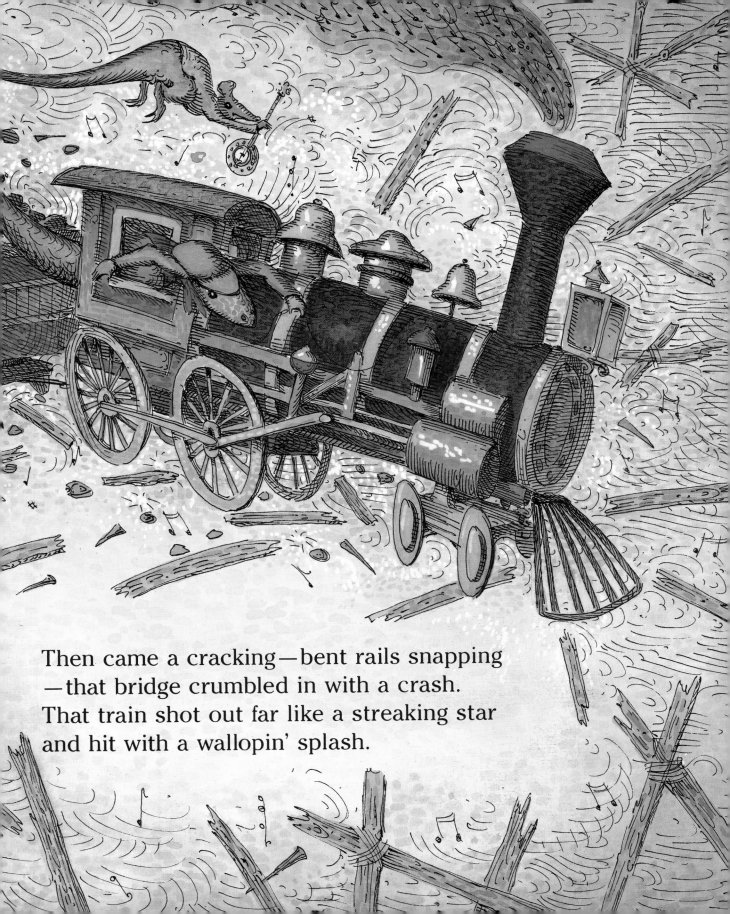

Then came a cracking—bent rails snapping
—that bridge crumbled in with a crash.
That train shot out far like a streaking star
and hit with a wallopin' splash.

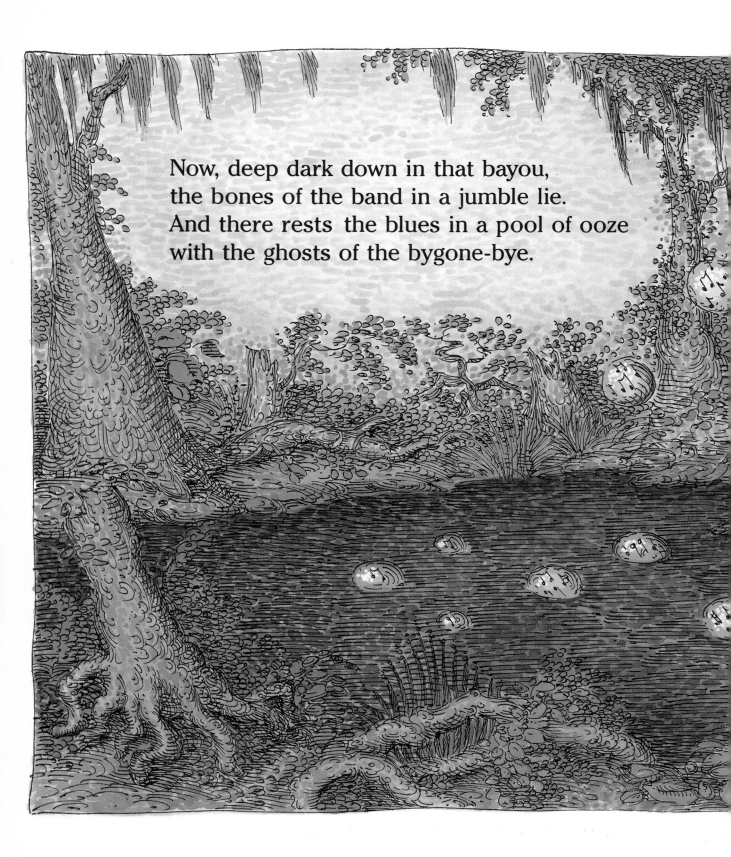

Now, deep dark down in that bayou,
the bones of the band in a jumble lie.
And there rests the blues in a pool of ooze
with the ghosts of the bygone-bye.

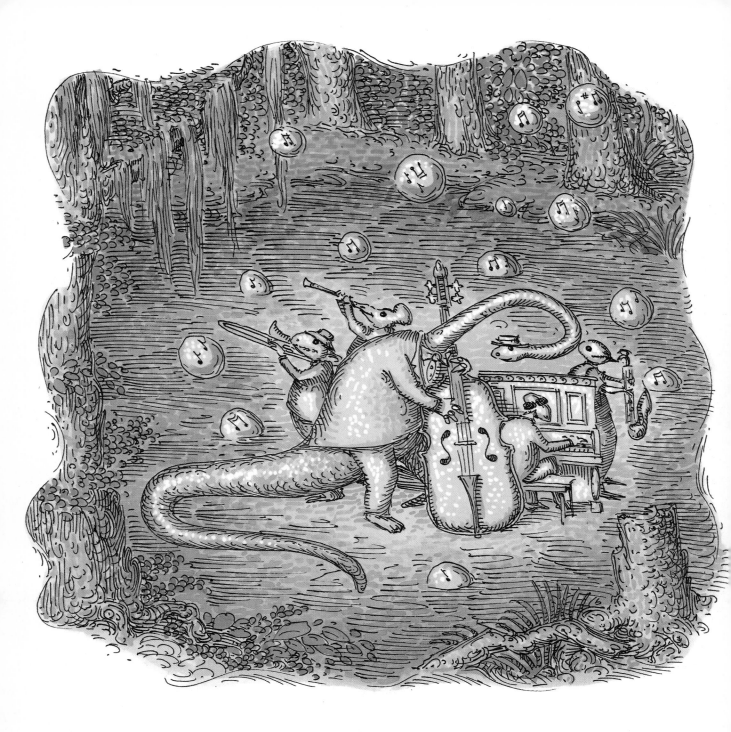

But that classic Jurassic blues is fantastic
and that bygone band's not gone.
There are folks who swear Billy's playing there
in that steamy bayou pond.